HEALER

A FANTASY ROMANCE

JODI KENDRICK

SOULGATE PUBLISHING

Dragon Island

Dragon Heat

Enchanted Ardor

Wish

EveL Worlds : FUCN'A

Tough Nut
Diamond in the Ruff
Honeyed Nut
Gorilla in the Hiss
FUCN'A Collection One
Pedigree Collection

Finely Aged

Dragon Steel

Global Paranormal Security Agency

Awakened
Surfacing
Polestar
Aquatic Investigations
Prowler

The Kindred Chronicles

Healer
Mercenary

The Soaring Dragon Chronicles

Return Flight
Changeling

ONE

Darya McLeighan sat back on her heels and blew the errant strands of copper hair away from her nose.

She crouched before an elder planted on her sturdy wooden stool. With his thread-worn work shirt raised, she inspected the wound on his side. His distinctive woodsy odour tickled her nose.

Her gaze flicked up to his face, wondering how in the Goddess' name he'd managed this one, this time.

Considering how best to broach the subject of his proud bachelor status and independence to ease him into the idea of finding a house mate—for safety's sake, she rose to her feet in search of the right herbs.

"Don't bother telling me I need someone to look after me, lass. I can see it all over yer face. If ye'd be obliged to just patch me up, I'll be back with a load of firewood for yer hearth."

"Alright, Elder Holtmann." She said as answer to both statements, smile hidden from him as she faced her wall of supplies.

Inspecting the crockery filling the shelves above the workbench, she pulled several down, setting them next to the mortar and pestle. She resumed her work, noting, again, that many of her pots were nearly empty. The one she needed most didn't even have residue left in it.

She glanced back at Elder Holtmann, who gazed out of the warbled glass of her front window.

Grinding the herbs together, she considered where else she could search for the desperately needed roots and flowers that couldn't be grown in her garden. Usually in the ancient woods and meadows beyond the swamp. They were getting harder to find.

Everything was getting harder to find.

Everything was just getting harder.

"Have you any news from the front?"

Elder Holtmann grunted. "I was figuring to ask ye the same. But last I heard, our troops were pushed back this way some, after the last skirmish. Back and forth they go."

Darya nodded.

His voice lightened. "I did hear of a new saddle-back merchant hereabouts."

"Saddle-back merchant?" she echoed, tapping the ground leaves into another vessel.

"Aye. He has a shop in the market town with his kin, but he rides out."

"A peddler."

"I suppose something of the sort."

"I wonder if he has assorted spoons." She said, glancing at the cluster of well-used utensils on the worktop.

"Spoons? Do ye not have sufficient supply with the ones I carved ye?"

She turned to Elder Holtmann. "Those are the finest spoons I have. But I need some of different materials. Not all wooden. Different qualities."

The old man nodded, satisfied his workmanship was acceptable. "I don't know nothing about that. But I do as ye say. Use the ash wood for mixing this. Or the willow spoon for mixing that. Exactly as ye say. I won't be wasting yer efforts each time ye patch me up."

She opened her mouth to speak, but he kept talking, squinting at her.

"I'll be visiting my nephew soon. I was thinking it was time to start teaching him more of what I know of the woods."

Her shoulders lowered. "That sounds like an excellent idea. And of course, he'd have to stay with you since his parents live on the far side of the village."

"Aye." He grunted. "Maybe ye should consider having someone stay with ye too, lass."

She smiled, letting the suggestion slip away. Darya had less interest in living with someone than the lifelong bachelor woodsman did.

Not anymore, anyway. Not since...

Shoving that particular memory away, she gathered medicines, and measured out several piles onto small linens, which she then folded and secured into a small pouch. She took up the last pile and began mixing it with boiled water from the hearth pot.

Darya selected the delicate spoon carved of crystal.

With another glance back at the elder, she confirmed his attention returned to the window. As quickly as she dared, she held her hands over the brew, fingers loose around the spoon. She closed her eyes and whispered to the Goddess, hoping she would overlook Darya's neglect of the temple—for the Elder's sake.

Hoping the magic would come. Hoping the Elder wouldn't see. Even an accidental slip of the tongue could have her re-conscripted.

Stop worrying about 'what ifs' *and focus on 'what* is.'

A moment later, the magic moved through her veins like ignited lava from her center toward her palms and fingertips.

She drew a deep, shuddering breath, trying to control the flare. A chill followed the sweep of heat, causing perspiration to prickle her skin.

The spoon warmed between her fingers as the magic flowed through it like a conduit. Tilting her hand, she dipped the spoon into the bowl, mixing and amplifying the brew's qualities.

There was little choice. She was missing the proper herbs to stave infections that would kill her patient. The medicine needed a little help to ensure the Elder's well being.

"Did ye say something, lass?"

"No, Elder, I was just counting to keep time." Her throat tightened on the lie.

With the medicine prepared, she clasped her hands together to ease the tremble.

Picking up the small bowl, she moved toward her patient.

On seeing her approach, he lifted the shirt he let fall earlier and arched to give her easier access.

"I appreciate what ye do for me, lass." His gruff voice was the softest she ever heard him speak. "We all do."

She looked up into his face, feeling the sincerity of his words. "Anytime. And I certainly appreciate all you do for me in return, Elder Holtmann. I seem to never be in want of firewood, or beautifully carved furniture or tools." She gently swiped the last of the paste over the wound and pressed a clean linen in place followed by bindings.

She stood hearing the rapid crunch of gravel just before her door burst open.

"Mistress, my Ma's time has come, and she needs ye," the boy said, breathless and wide-eyed.

Jeni.

Elder Holtmann patted her hand. "I'll see myself out."

She nodded and moved as quickly as she could, gathering what she needed. In her haste, she knocked the crystal spoon to the floor. Frustration flared through her as she noted the crack along the center, midway down the handle to the tip. Picking it up from the floor, she put it back on the counter where it separated at the split and toppled apart. A second later, she snatched it up and stuffed the pieces into her satchel with the smaller mortar and pestle she carried for visits, medicines and precious surgical knives.

Securing her supplies in the satchel, she followed the boy out of the house and up the long path to the main road. The unexpected appearance of a large warhorse carrying a well-dressed stranger at the intersection caused them to stumble back.

"Pardon, sir." Heart in throat, she huffed and hurried after the boy, barely giving the stranger another thought.

TWO

Nate Kirin patted Laoch's neck as he huffed and backed away from the woman who suddenly appeared from behind a lilac bush, followed by a red-faced boy.

"Pardon, Sir." She said, glancing at Laoch's hooves and substantial girth as she skirted around them.

"Mistress McLeighan?" He called after her, twisting in his saddle.

"Come back tomorrow." She shouted over her shoulder without stopping or sparing him a glance.

Laoch took two steps forward when he pranced back again. A grizzled old man appeared in the narrow road from behind the same bush.

"Master Kirin." He tipped his head respectfully.

"Good day Elder Holtmann." They exchanged several pleasantries.

The old man eyed him for a moment. "I reckon the mistress would see ye back tomorrow as she said if ye'd a mind to return. And if ye have a supply of medicines—and spoons. Not the wooden kind." He turned to continue on his way, opposite the direction Mistress McLeighan travelled, but the same that Nate faced.

Nate dismounted Laoch's back, sliding a hand over his neck. "I'll walk with you, Elder."

"I wouldn't want to hold ye up, but I would appreciate any news."

"If you tell me of Mistress's healing skills, I'd be glad to."

Elder Holtmann's squint-eyed assessment gave Nate pause. "What do ye wish to know of the Mistress?" Suspicion tightened the grizzled face.

"I came to offer my wares, but I also came to ask her for help. My aunt has been ailing."

"The widow that runs the shop?"

Nate nodded.

The old man's eyes bore into him as they made their way slowly down the road. His gnarled hand rested on his side. "Mistress McLeighan's off to deliver a babe. Likely back tomorrow if all goes well."

Nate waved a hand toward the protective posture. "Did she patch you up?"

The old man lowered his hand. "Aye, and a good job of it, she did. Always does. She's been a boon to us, hereabouts these last couple of years."

"She isn't native born then?"

The old man shrugged.

Nate ignored his shrewd gaze. The woodsman's scrutiny rivaled that of any admiral he'd served under.

"She appeared one day. And began helping anyone that needed it. She's one of us, even if she isn't from here." A moment later, he added. "We suspect she was avoiding a bad husband that oughtn't come looking for her. Anyone that were to mean her harm would have to answer to the likes of me, and I keep my axes sharp."

"It's good she has your protection. One never knows, especially with the increased raids."

"Have we lost the line again? They always grow bolder when they push us back to our own territory."

"Aye." He sighed. "The back and forth is endless and meaningless."

The old man's head jerked in his direction. "Did ye serve?"

"I did. Was ready to give my life for the Empire. Nearly did too. If I hadn't been carried off the field and patched up, I'd be buried four feet under the muck and ruin of the old western crop fields north of Green Valley village." Nate rubbed a thumb over the leather strap of Laoch's reins in his hand as they walked.

"I remember when that valley was prosperous. The breadbasket of our region."

"I'm sorry to say that I was part of its ruin. Like much else around here."

"No longer had the taste for it, did ye?"

"Honourably discharged after that last incident. Handed some medals, a pat on the head and offered a political position."

"Politics." The old man spat.

Nate chuckled. "Not my arena. Thought it best I just go home before they realize that and kick me out anyway."

"Got to keep yer horse."

"He came with me, there was no way he wasn't leaving with me."

The old man's scrutiny returned, but he said nothing more on the matter. "This here be the path to my home. I part ways with ye, sir. But remember, as I said, the mistress be in need of spoons and medicines if ye have some."

The rapid beat of feet on the road behind them drew their attention as a boy—the same boy raced toward them.

"Oy! Tommy!" The old man yelled, slowing the boy. "Where's mistress?"

"Raiders!"

"Ye left her alone?" Holtmann barked like any experienced general.

"She's hidden. She bade me run for help and supplies. I'm to alert the militia. She couldn't find the herbs she would need for Ma along the way," he panted.

Nate shifted Laoch's reins in his hands as he turned to face the boy. "Take my horse to the militia, then go to my shop for what she needs. She gave you a list to recite?"

The boy nodded, listing off the various roots and herbs.

"I have some of those in my saddlebags." Nate removed a sling bag from a pack and began moving carefully wrapped packages from the saddlebag to the sling bag with quick, precise movements. "Last I heard, the militia were out on patrol. They may be on the far side of the region, but they will have a man in the village. Go there first. Then to my shop. I will find Mistress McLeighan. I don't have everything she needs, so it's important you get the rest. My aunt will give you anything you need when she sees you with Laoch."

The boy eyed Laoch, weary, and not making any move to get closer.

"I doubt the lad's been on any horse, let alone a beast of war such as yers." The old man said, his voice heavy with concern.

"He's well trained, you've nothing to fear." Nate pulled the wide-eyed boy closer so he could help him mount and placed the reins in his hands. "With ease," he said as the boy's hands clutched the leather in a death grip.

"Where did ye leave her, Tommy?" Elder Holtmann demanded.

Tommy's eyes glistened. "I didn't mean to leave her—I wouldn't have, but she made me go."

"Of course, she did, so ye could get help, and ye have," Holtmann said.

"Where is she, Tommy?"

"We went off the road soon after leaving. We cut to the west woods to find the herbs she needed. But there weren't any." He gulped.

Nate patted Tommy's knee. The boy, with unruly red hair and a freckled face, couldn't be more than ten or eleven years. "Is there a landmark I can look for that will lead me to her?"

"The abandoned apple orchard, by a cluster of Lilac bushes in bloom. But she won't stay there if it's safe. She said she'd get to my Ma. She promised. Ma needs her."

"I'll find her and get this medicine to her for your Mother. Go to the militia outpost in the village, then to my shop in the market. What I have will help but isn't enough."

Tommy turned uncertain eyes to Elder Holtmann.

"It's good Tommy, do as he says."

Laoch's ear twitched as Nate whispered to him. "To the village. Be swift and keep him safe."

The war horse bobbed his head. As soon as Nate patted his flank, he took off.

Tommy teetered atop the horse, but managed to hold on.

"Ye don't have a sword." The old man said to Nate. "I have axes plenty."

Nate shook his head. "I'm not a soldier anymore. I've no use for weapons."

Holtmann's expression turned incredulous. "I thought ye were a man of sense.

What soldier-trained man doesn't carry a weapon on the frontier?"

Nate grinned. "Lost my sense long ago. No time for that particular story right now if I'm to get these medicines to Mistress McLeighan in good time. I will see to her safety. You'd best prepare in case those raiders visit your property or head for the village."

"Aye, if ye make it alive. I'll be ready. Good fortune to ye," the elder said, watching as Nate turned in the direction Tommy ran from.

"Sharpen your axes," Nate called as he began jogging.

"They're always sharp." Holtmann called back. "Not like yer wits."

THREE

D arya held her breath, ears straining to hear over the hush of wind through the lilac bushes that surrounded her. Ignoring the buzzing, hungry mosquitoes hovering around her head and ears, she waited and watched through the branches.

She was sure Tommy got away unseen. She just prayed he didn't run into a split arm of the raiding party. They were usually larger than this group. As ragged as they were, she hoped this was all they could afford to send across the vaporous border.

The military trained her to wait out scouts. To be still in hiding. If she died, her patient died. That's what the head of the military medical unit taught them.

The urgency to save a life in need pushed at her from the inside out. Still, she forced herself to wait.

Tommy's mother, Jeni, needed her. Darya delivered Jeni's previous child and aided her through the heartbreaking miscarriage of another. It was going to be a very long night. If she could get there. Even if she did, they both knew there were no assurances. Not when it came to birthing.

The odds were as precarious as any battlefield she'd worked on, with the likes of which much nobler as it was in the service of pure life, and not death dealing.

Her hands gripped the strap of the satchel slung across her chest, tossing aside those memories to focus on evading the raiders and help Jeni.

Easing out of the foliage, she scanned the clearing and orchard. There was no sign of the band of men. She dashed for the nearby wall of pines that held the forest back from the orchard. Casting glances and trying to listen above the sounds of her own footfalls and racing heart, she made her way toward the creek.

There were still missing medicines to search out and collect. She had to raise Jeni's odds.

Yes, Darya could use magic to heal the woman, but even that was never assured. Especially lately. Hands gripping the satchel again, as much to ensure she still possessed it as to still the tremble in her hands, she dashed again.

She moved along the creek, where trees were sparse, and the terrain was almost open below the dense overhead branches still struggling to bud at this time of year. She twisted and turned on the spot, searching for the splash of colour she needed.

There!

Launching forward, she whispered and dropped to her knees beside the tiny plant next to the creek bed. "Thank Goddess."

She hesitated only a second.

There was only one, and it was underdeveloped. Her desperation decided its fate.

Digging, the scents of fresh growth, old rot and damp earth rose from the opening she'd created in the soil. She carefully freed the plant from the forest's layers amid the thick pine roots and terricolous lichen-covered stones. Searching out the linens in her satchel, she wrapped and slid it among the other medicines. Some things couldn't be grown in her little garden.

She rinsed her hands in the rushing creek water, which eased the tremble in her fingers.

Too late, she realized the sound of the rushing water masked any other sounds in the forest as she was hauled to her feet.

"What's this here?"

She was spun to face a dirty, gap-toothed man who stank of rancid sweat and rotted gums. Her eyes quickly darted to the four other faces that formed an arc around her.

"I'm a healer. Please. I have to aid in the delivery of a child."

"What will you do for me if I let you go on your merry way?" His hot, foul breath wormed its way up her nostrils.

"She might be a witch, Willem. Don't play around with her."

His hand tightened on her arm. She swallowed the cry of pain, staring up into his face.

He grinned.

Her stomach lurched.

She scanned the faces again. There were at least two that regarded her with uncertain expressions. One was disinterested. The last seemed as intent as her captor.

"We don't have much time. Either kill her or let her go." The disinterested one said. "They won't wait for us, and we don't know where the enemy militia is."

Willem grunted, gaze never leaving her face. "You go on ahead, I'll catch up."

"Willem don't mess with her, she could be dangerous."

"You're wasting time." One other said.

She listened as they debated among themselves. The fearful ones turned away, seeming to not want any part of what Willem had in mind.

If she was fast enough, she just might make it. Her free hand slipped into her bag, searching for the small knives she used for surgeries. Her fingertip caught on the jagged edge of the broken spoon.

Fingers wrapped around it, she withdrew her hand and struck lightning fast.

Willem dropped to his knees, gurgling, the crystal handle protruding from his neck. She wrenched it free, slick with the spray of his blood, then turned and ran through the creek.

She would only have a few seconds before the others shook off their shock.

She gained a hundred yards before a hand clamped on the back of her shirt. Darya spun, swinging, not caring which of the men it was so long as she dropped them.

She had to get to Jeni.

The raider dodged her swing and struck her. The blow impacted the side of her face, sending her to the ground. Her ears rang and vision swam. Her foot shot up, connecting with soft tissues. He fell with a grunt and a hard wheeze. Grabbing a rock, she brought it down on his head. She didn't know if she killed him or not when he fell sideways, eyes closed. Her chest heaved as she stared at him a few seconds longer, watching for movement.

Looking up, another figure joined the remaining three raiders, seeming to hold them at bay.

She blinked. A large, well-dressed man stood between her and the attackers, stance wide, hands empty, hovering before him. He stood ready, between the raiders and herself, facing the imminent threat.

Dropping her gaze to the man at her feet, she saw there was a knife tied at his belt and wrenched it free.

The newcomer glanced back in her direction, calling out. "Mistress." He unslung a bag similar to hers from across his chest and tossed it in her direction. "Take this and go to Tommy's mother."

Her breath shuddered through her.

Tommy must have found help.

The newcomer appeared to be unarmed.

Sticky, broken spoon in one hand, enemy weapon in the other, she strode toward the stranger, facing the three remaining raiders as one of them rushed forward.

The stranger twisted, somehow using the force and momentum of the armed attacker to send him sailing through the air, landing with the distinct crack of bone.

The attacker didn't move.

The two remaining raiders glanced wide-eyed at the stranger, then to Darya. She still clutched the bloodied shard in one hand and the dead man's knife in the other.

"Witch." One squeaked, backing away. The other followed suit. Both rushed away from her, through the forest, casting backward glances.

Three bodies littered the forest floor. While she was sure Willem wasn't still alive, she couldn't be certain of the other two. They were at least unconscious for now.

"Thank you." She reached for the discarded bag.

He turned as she was about to take off.

She froze, eyes locked on the blood staining his clothes. "Are you wounded?"

"I'll be fine, get to Tommy's mother."

Darya surveyed the growing wet patch. He wasn't fine. Her eyes flicked to the raider he'd toppled, stained short sword fallen next to him.

She straightened. "I'm Darya McLeighan, sir. Please remove your shirt."

FOUR

N ate grinned, recognizing the medic protocol. He heard it enough times. But he was a civilian now and couldn't resist the urge to tease. "Mistress McLeighan, there is no need to reward me for my gallantry. I shall keep my clothing as it is."

She squinted at him, then frowned.

He held his breath, unsure if she was about to reprimand his forward comment, or if she finally recognized him. Facing her, his pulse was wilder now than during the recent scuffle with the brigands.

She studied his face for a long moment, uncertainty flickering across her lovely features.

Does she remember me?

He searched her face as she scanned the forest with grey eyes tipped up at the outer corners. Freckles sprinkled across the bridge of her nose and flushed cheeks. Her plump lips parted as she huffed.

"Sir, I have a labouring woman to attend. The sooner I see to your wounds, the sooner I can help her birth her child safely."

Disappointment twisted in his chest, even as relief escaped with a huff. He hadn't been sure she'd recognize him after so long. After the circumstances. After all, how many wounded had she tended during her years of service. What was one more fallen soldier?

Still, he held a spark of hope she'd recognize his voice. It was nice to speak to her without the itch of bandages covering his face.

"It's not deep, it can wait."

"Wait increases the chance of infection."

Of course, he knew that. He also knew she wouldn't let it go, especially not after his interference. And that healers wouldn't walk away from a patient in need if they didn't have to.

Impatience to leave compressed her lips.

He stepped toward her, removing his surcoat and tunic. The blood oozed toward the waistband of his trousers. The flesh and muscle around the wound throbbed, threatening to steal his breath away.

He felt her gaze like butterfly wings, fluttering over his torso, lingering over old scars, then resting on the fresh wound. Assessing. Impersonal.

She still hasn't really *looked at my face*.

Her gaze remained honed on the wound, hands working through her satchel for what she needed.

Steady and sure, she cleaned the gash.

Nate remained still, drawing deep, even breaths, controlling the urge to flinch and gasp with every sharp pain. The familiar, bitter odour of antiseptic herbs cloyed at his nostrils and coated his tongue.

Then she hesitated, her eyes flicking between the still oozing wound and his chin.

It was deeper than he insinuated.

"I've only one *slànachadh bodhaig* flower that I managed to find right before the raiders attacked. I'll need it for the birthing."

Her breath hitched. "I can use it to stave off infection and fever and hope to find another on the way."

Nate placed a hand over hers, hovering between them. "Keep it for your patient. She'll need it far more than I do. It would be faster to use magic."

Her head jerked up, eyes riveted to his face.

"How-" She swallowed, studying his face more closely, then swept his scarred torso. "You're a soldier. Of course."

His thumb brushed the back of her hand. "Mistress, I'm more than just a soldier. Granted, it has been a long time and-"

"Good Goddess! General Kirin!" Her hands dropped, and she snapped upright. Her eyes studied him hard, her brow furrowed. "What are you doing out here? Never mind, of course I'll use magic to heal your wound." She said, extending her fingers toward him.

He allowed her to approach and focus on the task at hand while he found another way to broach the subject he really wanted to.

Was now the time? Perhaps it wasn't. They were in the middle of the forest and she needed to tend to a patient.

"Don't expend too much of your energy, Mistress, just stop the bleeding and hold your reserves."

She gave a sharp nod.

His skin at the wound site itched as her magic ignited the healing process.

The sensation, the sight of her head bent over her work, was achingly familiar.

"They say when someone uses magic on you, they leave something of themselves behind."

The heat flowing from her fingers stuttered. She clenched her fingers into fists for a few seconds, then opened them to continue.

"That's enough." He said, voice soft, pulling his shirt back over his head. "Is the house far?"

"I'm more than halfway there. Thank you for the supplies. You'll see that Tommy makes it home safely? Those raiders look like they're bound for the village."

"He's safe atop my horse and headed for the militia outpost. They'll be alerted. He'll meet us after he goes to my shop to collect the rest of the supplies I didn't have with me."

Her eyes narrowed, then widened. "You're the saddle-back peddler. That was you that almost ran us over with that war horse."

"I prefer merchant, but yes, that was me. I was about to call on you when you ran out in front of Laoch. Lucky he's well trained and didn't trample you. You really ought to look before running into the road like that."

"I-" her lips snapped shut. "Aye, General Kirin."

"I'm no longer a General. Move on."

Her brow lifted at the order, but she turned and began walking.

FIVE

Darya's heart hammered in her chest.

General Kirin!

Of all the people to appear in the middle of the forest delivering medical supplies, he's the last I could have imagined.

The handsome, beloved charismatic hero of the empire, General Kirin, now a saddle-back merchant.

She shook her head.

No one will believe it. I'm not sure I *believe it.*

But the sense of familiarity eased the prickle at the back of her neck.

It made her chest ache, recalling another man, another time.

A man I could have given 'forever' to.

Now she understood where she recognized his voice.

Darya had tended the General on the battlefield over the years before he'd gone missing and presumed dead. That was shortly before her term of service finally finished. The worst battle either side had seen before or since. So many lost. The clearing stations overflowed with wounded. The morgue tents...

She drew a deep breath and eased it out, letting go of the memories before they could crash over her, overwhelming her senses.

I no longer serve the military. The Emperor.

Her pace increased. She lost time and still needed to scan for more *sàbhaladh beatha* or *slànachadh bodhaig* flowers. Jeni still waited for her.

Clenching her fists, she prayed to the Goddess as she walked. Not that the goddess would pay her much attention. Not since Darya turned away from her in those final days of service and neglected to pay her respects in the temples.

I just hope I have enough magic in me to help Jeni through this delivery.

The flow of magic was weak when tending Elder Holtmann and sputtered while healing the General.

She glanced at him from the corner of her eye, drawing her thoughts again.

He's still a handsome man.

Deeply preoccupied with her mission to get to Jeni's side, she'd paid little attention to the physical attributes of the man who'd risked his life to save her. Heal the wounded, tend the sick, nothing else mattered.

Focus on the work.

This is my life.

A powerful general turned humble merchant.

Unable to shake the curiosity, she said, "what happened to you?"

It was a blunt, bold question. Insubordinate. Impertinent. But he said he was no longer a General. And she was no longer a military healer.

"Our soldiers nearly lost the battle when you disappeared from the battlefield," she said.

"Seriously wounded. Almost died. Almost."

She turned to look at him, at the rasp of his voice. Studying him again, that prickle of familiarity washed over her. She couldn't fathom it. She'd tended him once or twice, but not enough to merit this kind of strangeness. "You've barely any scars. Your medic was very skilled."

"The best." His voice dropped again, the sound pulling at her. His eyes remained on hers.

They say when someone uses magic on you; they leave something of themselves behind.

A shiver rippled through her. She heard someone say that once before. Someone she spent a lot of time with in the clearing station. A foot soldier nearly lost to the greedy mud and blood of the battlefield after severe wounds to the head and face when an incendiary weapon hit his line.

The hairs on her body rose.

The reminder brought with it loneliness' ruthless grip around her heart. She resumed walking, shoving the memory of *that* particular soldier from her mind. There was no time for heart ache.

SIX

A squat cottage came into view. Nate breathed a sigh of relief, resisting the urge to rub at the itching wound.

He glanced at Darya preceding him to the stone well and drew fresh water.

If she recognized who he really was, she gave no indication.

Would she be angry?

He wouldn't blame her.

He withheld his identity all that time. All those weeks at the clearing station, head bound in bandages after the incendiary knocked him out flat.

The event flashed through his memory, causing him to grit his teeth and ride out the wave of fear and anguish and recall of pain.

Nate was dragged from his saddle, and separated from his warhorse, Laoch, for the first time in the history of their relationship. Surrounded by overwhelming odds, he fought alongside his men. His own side launched the incendiary. Knocked to the ground, an enemy soldier trying hard to put his sword in Nate's throat took the brunt of the explosion. Dragged from the field once the fighting eased, he remembered little else. Not until he'd awakened more fully to the sounds and smells of the clearing station.

Injured soldiers moaning, sometimes screaming. The bitter scents of cleaning solutions, strong but not strong enough to erase the tang of blood and burnt flesh.

Medic Darya McLeighan was one of the healers posted to his corner of the ward. For weeks. Healed, men and women in neighbouring beds were sent home or back into the field. Many died beyond the ability of the magic and medicines.

I was nearly one of them.

But something about Mistress McLeighan's voice held him fast. Kept him wanting to remain in his body. Wanting to fight for life.

Even before the event, he'd begun to lose hope, though he gave no indication.

What were we fighting for?

He was so very tired of fighting.

But he had no right to walk away, not when thousands of foot soldiers, conscripted, forced to the battlefield, were not so privileged.

He continued for *them*. Fought for *them*.

Until I couldn't anymore.

He breathed deeply of the pine and early spring air surrounding them, anchoring himself in the present for a few seconds.

Dismissing the memories, Nate stepped forward, taking the water bucket from Mistress McLeighan's hands. "Go on." He nodded toward the front door of the cottage. "I'm not so wounded I can't manage a bucket of water."

Approaching the door, she gave a sharp knock, calling out before easing the door open. "Jeni, it's Darya."

Nate followed her inside. The cottage was dark, the air stale and heavy with age-old smells of burning wood and peat, cooked food and general human life. The late day sun barely reached several feet past the warbled glass of the windows. Not enough to illuminate Mistress McLeighan's patient, propped on the cot in the back corner of the single room home.

Mistress McLeighan removed the satchels, placed them on the table and immediately moved toward the bed where a woman, nearly lost beneath piled quilts, panted.

Tiny in stature; she seemed to be all belly. She reached out, seeking Darya's hand.

"Jeni." Darya said, dropping to her knees next to the woman and began pushing the coverings aside to expose the rounded abdomen. "Where are the other children?"

"I sent them to my sister when Tommy went to fetch you."

Darya nodded as her hands moved over the woman's distended stomach, pressing firm but gentle fingers. "We'll send for them after you've delivered the baby. I'll have to look inside." She said, voice soft.

Jeni nodded.

Darya got to her feet and moved toward the hearth, where a cauldron of hot water stood ready.

Nate set the bucket of fresh water nearby.

Darya washed her hands and began preparations.

"I'm at your service, Mistress McLeighan." He said, standing aside, well out of her way.

She looked up at him and nodded. "Without Tommy here, I will need the help, sir."

"Nate."

The strain on her face eased. "Nate. Darya."

SEVEN

Despite his lack of experience in birthing, the General followed Darya's implicit instructions. Jeni had already been in labour for some time before their arrival. Her body ready. Darya made her tea from the supplies from Nate's satchel to ease the strain and help her conserve her energy. She would need it when the pushing started.

For now, hours later, Jeni slipped into a brief sleep between contractions. Darya bathed the sweat from Jeni's brow and neck, providing some little comfort in a highly uncomfortable situation. "Jeni, I'm going to fetch more water from the well. I'll just be outside the door. I'll hear if you call."

Jeni nodded, weak, giving Darya's hand a light squeeze.

Nate grasped the well bucket before she reached for it. They went out together.

"She'll be alright?" he asked, tethering the bucket with the rope to lower it.

Darya stretched her back, face turned to the stars just visible between the tree-tops surrounding the cottage. She breathed deeply of the sweet forest air. "The child is turned in the correct position. Jeni is small and her births are hard and long but she is strong. The concern will be if there is a rupture. Bleeding is always the hardest to combat. Especially internal." Her attention returned to Nate's face.

"I recall the clearing stations and the odds." He hauled the refilled bucket back up to the surface. "What can I do?"

Darya's eyes studied him in the dim light. "You've provided supplies. But I only have one *slànachadh bodhaig* plant that is un-derdeveloped. I don't know if it will be enough."

"Can't your magic magnify its qualities?"

She nodded. "Aye, but my magic is de-pleted. It has been for some time. I'm not sure it will be enough." Her gaze dropped to the refilled water bucket. "The well is nearly dry, so-to-speak." She gave a weak laugh.

"And you used some of your energy to heal me this afternoon."

Her eyes flicked back to his face. "As it should be. If you hadn't intervened, and brought the needed supplies, I'd not be here at all." She studied him another moment and smiled. "General Kirin. Saddle-back Merchant. How did you end up outside my house?"

"You have quite the reputation in the area. I was coming to ask for your help. And see if you needed any wares, of course."

"Help?"

"My aunt has been ill with rheumatism for some time. I thought you could help her, knowing how skilled you are."

Her brow lifted. "Good military medical training."

"I recall. And you healed so many that would have been lost."

"I did my duty."

Disappointment skittered across his features, gone just as quickly as it appeared.

"As did you." She said, her voice stern yet soft. She drew another deep breath. "So many of us gave all that we had to duty. So much so that there was almost nothing left. Recovery—healing is a long, slow process. For those that provide it as well."

"How do you replenish the energy? Rest?"

"Usually that does it. But it's more in the daily joy of things. Finding peace or wonder or love. Or all of those things. Each person is different."

"Which is it for you?"

"I don't know. But what I'm doing now isn't working. And the thought of being unable to help—to use my gifts to help others... I'll be useless."

"A healer unable to heal is like a fighter unable to lift a sword when the enemy is near."

Darya recalled Nate's actions in the forest. "You did well enough without a sword."

"Aside from getting wounded in the process." He reminded her. "Why wasn't your man travelling with you? Where is he?"

Caught off guard by the direct question, she deflected it. "I've always been on my own. Why were you unarmed? I never would have imagined a soldier, let alone a General would ever be parted from their weapon."

"After seeing the devastation on the battlefield for so long. Leading so many to their deaths. Watching the unending cycles of wounded and burden of healing in the clearing stations. And to what end? What was it all for? I couldn't do it anymore. Be responsible for the deaths of so many."

Darya had wondered the same. It was why she hadn't engaged in another cycle of duty. Why she kept her magic hidden. So that she wouldn't be conscripted and forced back into indenture. Because that's what happens. If you don't volunteer, you're conscripted.

"I won't waste the efforts of my healer and willfully engage in acts of violence."

"They must have been quite impactful on you. I hear it takes a lot to impress a war-hardened general."

"Aye, she did." He smiled as his eyes slid over her face.

Something about the way he looked at her made her heart and stomach flutter. He was a handsome man. Many other healers spoke of him during quiet times. The famous General Kirin. Fierce soldier, handsome as sin, and held the world in his palm.

Now that the immediate danger of the raiders and the urgency to reach Jeni was past, there was time to breathe and think. And admire the strong build and sensual smile of the man beside her.

"Was it Elian? I recall her skill. And she was quite the beauty. Many of the soldiers sent her love letters after they left the clearing station. Very popular among the convalescents."

"I don't recall a Mistress Elian." He said. His gaze fixed on her lips, then swept the rest of her face.

His expression tripped her pulse, awakening some dormant, locked away and buried part of her that was more than a medic—more than a healer. A woman with long-ignored desires.

"Darya?" Jeni's voice drew their attention.

"I'm here," Darya said, instantly moving toward the open door of the cottage.

Nate followed close behind with the fresh water.

Secure that lock, Darya. Now isn't the time to spin fantasies about the Emperor's favourite General.

EIGHT

Nate responded to every one of Darya's orders.

She was a flurry of movement in the small house.

He did his best to stay out of her way and move the instant she required something of him. Boil more water, wash soiled linens, hang the washed linens to dry, grind more herbs, boil more water...

On your way to being a General, you learn how to take orders so that you may learn how to give them.

I've always been on my own.

On her own. No mate. Alone. Like himself. It gave him some hope, in so much that she was not already promised to another, perhaps?

He'd been about to turn down the path to her house for many reasons that day.

Help for his aunt and the offer of supplies was the logical reasons to go.

The excuses.

But the true reason was to see her again. To determine if those weeks in the clearing station were still valid in his heart.

He recalled the long hours where she would sit with him during the worst of it. Her kindness and gentle hands. The bloom of her magic. The frequency of it left its signature in his flesh and blood and bones after so long under her direct care.

She hadn't known who he was during that time. They brought him in, unidentified, face damaged and bandaged. He nearly slipped into the abyss, but her voice had been a drifting tether in the void, then an anchor. Then finally a hoist.

He watched her now, tending to Jeni with the same care and compassion she'd tended to him. And the thousands of other soldiers. He was no different to her than any other patient.

But to him, she was *his* world for weeks and weeks until they moved him to another ward to recover.

A high-ranking General, injured and unidentified. A patient like all the others.

In those weeks of pain, there'd been freedom. He never told them who he was because he needed to decide once he realized he wasn't ready to die just yet.

From that clearing station, he saw the cost of this constant battle on the border. The battle for dominance. The whim of their Emperor leagues and leagues from the fighting, safely ensconced in the heart of the empire.

He served his time. They all served their time. Done their duty.

But this Emperor, whom he met many times, pushed his little pieces across his map, chest puffed like a boy playing soldier with wooden bits.

So he could have more land.

For the people, he said.

The people living along that border hadn't wanted it, for the people living across that arbitrary border were friends and family.

"The child has crowned." Darya said.

A spark of fear bloomed in his chest. He smothered it, as the military trained him to do. He was not in command of this mission.

Nate moved closer to Jeni's head. "What do I do?"

"Give me your hand." The words ground through Jeni's clenched teeth.

"I shouldn't be witnessing this intimate moment, Madam."

She gripped his hand, harder than any man's grasp three times her size. "I don't care!" she screamed, bearing down.

Decency dictated Nate should look away from Jeni's exposed calves.

Glancing up at his face, Darya pulled Jeni's nightdress to her spread knees, shielding his view of what happened beyond.

Darya spoke, steady and calm, instructing and encouraging.

Nate stood in wonder, hand going numb. The intimacy of the situation was not lost on him as Jeni moaned through another contraction.

The lives of so many men had hinged on the tip of his orders dealing death—to his men or those across the line of engagement. Us or them. Death to someone.

He never before witnessed the miracle of life being brought forward. The effort, the danger. He had no control, none of them did.

Where is her partner? He should be here, not I.

He held fast to Jeni's hand as she panted.

How hard it was for this small woman to bring life to this one child.

And how easy it was for each life to be extinguished.

He grappled for so long over his choice to leave his post. No matter what he said to his superiors, whether or not they agreed, it was the Emperor's will. They were just conduits for his wishes.

Nate no longer wanted to be part of it. Couldn't be. He allowed them to believe he was no longer fit for service.

He walked away from violence. Too many men died at his command.

Surely, I have some other purpose?

The communication between Darya and Jeni continued with encouragement to breathe, to push through the increased contractions and to relax in the seconds in between.

Hand still clasped by Jeni's, full of pins and needles, the muscle and bone bruised as she screamed through the final push.

Realizing his own breathing was as laboured as Jeni's, Nate drew a slow, calming breath. The musky tang of blood and afterbirth filled the small cottage, hanging in the enclosed space.

He stared in wonder as Darya cleaned and swaddled the child, the baby's face tight as it wailed. How hard the effort of birth must have been for this little one, too.

Jeni finally released his hand to accept the infant being placed on her chest.

Darya returned to work and issued more orders, drawing his attention from the little face.

He moved as directed. They weren't finished.

Jeni exposed a breast to feed the little one as Darya worked to help her body complete the afterbirth process. Nate helped clear it all away.

Soiled linens into more herb-infused boiled water.

Finally, Darya put the clean, dry linens in place and pulled the blanket up over Jeni and the child. They fell to exhaustion.

"They'll rest for a time. While they do, I must clean up and prepare the *slànachadh bodhaig* flower to help her heal." She said, her voice low so as not to disturb her patients.

Dark smudges under her eyes accented her lack of sleep.

"I've always thought you were incredible, Mistress Darya. Now I know you're simply wondrous."

She blinked, lips parting as though to speak, but having no response, she closed them again with a hint of a smile and nodded her thanks.

He helped her clean up.

Again, they went out to the well, Darya carrying the empty bucket.

Nate took it from her fingers, lowered it into the well, and drew it up again. This time, he reached for the nearby ladle and offered Darya some of the fresh water. She leaned forward to sip.

Eyes closed, she sighed.

Nate drank the cool water and dipped the ladle back into the bucket to replenish it, and offered it again to Darya.

She drank more. "Thank you."

Once they were both finished, he refilled the bucket and set it on the stone rim of the well.

"What happens now?"

"I have to monitor the bleeding. If it doesn't slow to a normal state, then she'll need help. As I've said before, I have the one *slànachadh bodhaig* flower which will help, but I don't know that it's enough. My magic is almost drained, and I've broken the crystal spoon that magnifies it when it's weak. If things turn in the wrong direction, I don't know if I can save her."

Nate recalled the translucent shard she used to defend herself against the raider in the forest. "It was among the listed items you told Tommy to bring back."

She nodded. "It's a rare item, but I had to hope there could be one at the shop."

"I don't think there is, Darya. But there may be some *sàbhaladh beatha* root stocked." He said.

"That is good. I'll prepare it when Tommy returns. Just in case."

"My aunt will have insisted he wait until sunup. Especially with the raiders in the countryside. If he's unable to make it back to us in time, how do I help you replenish your magic if you need to use it?"

She shrugged. "I don't know, to be honest."

Nate stared at her.

"Not anymore."

He was quiet for a long moment, looking up at the dark sky and their peaceful surroundings. "What would you want most for yourself?"

"A family." She said immediately.

Her voice was so quiet it was almost lost on the hush of the gentle breeze through the spring leaves.

"I lost most of mine when I was young to the border skirmishes. My brother and sister and I survived because we weren't home, but our parents and other siblings were brutally taken from us."

"Where are they now?"

"My sister is always off on adventures. I tease her about how mercenary she is, and she doesn't deny it. She is a true Kindred to her core. My brother is employed among the palace guard at the capital. We don't see each other as often as we would like. What of yourself?"

Nate shrugged. "Just my widowed aunt. Parents taken young too. No siblings."

"No wife and little ones?"

He shook his head. "Never had the time. Didn't give it much thought until-" he glanced at her open expression, smiled and let the words stay unfinished.

"Until what?" she smiled, pushing him with her elbow.

His gaze dropped to that simple, playful contact that rippled through him. He lifted his eyes to her open smile.

"I've missed that smile, Mistress Darya. The memory of it has stayed with me since the first time I saw you smile at one of your patients."

She blinked, gaze moving to the well then back to his face, her confusion clear. "I don't recall smiling in the presence of the great General Kirin. That would be unprofessional and frowned upon by the military medical corps."

"It's alright." He leaned toward her and said in a loud whisper. "I won't tell of your unwitting lapse, because you didn't know there was a General to be on guard about."

"What do you mean?" she said, clearly amused by the mystery.

"You kept me alive for weeks. Forced me back to life when I was ready to let go. That smile of yours..." what could he say? He searched for the words in the night's darkness, among the hushed trees and sleeping wildlife. The transitional hour between night and day. The stillness, the late hour, the exhaustion, the seclusion. The intimacy of the moment eased the self-restraint to keep those words to himself.

The fear of her rejection.

He'd been going to see her for this moment. It just got shifted so that it wasn't working out in the same way he imagined.

"General?"

His gaze shot back to her lovely face, so full of concern.

"Are you unwell?"

He searched her features. A bruise began to blossom on the side of her face from the hit she'd taken in the forest. Loose strands of copper hair framed her face, softening her expression. He lifted his hand and gently tucked an errant strand behind her ear, breath held lest she reject the intimacy of such an action.

She didn't. Her brows rose. "General Kirin, I don't recall spending much time with you beyond the quick summons to heal a few wounds before you returned to the battlefield." She shook her head. "Surely you're confusing me with someone else."

"No. Mistress, I could never confuse you with another." His thumb grazed her chin, his gaze found her mouth again.

"Then?" she prompted for an explanation; her breath hitched between parted lips.

"The bandaged soldier. The incendiary."

Her brows rose a little higher, as recognition replaced the confusion. Tears filled her eyes. She blinked them away. "That was you?"

He nodded.

"Why didn't you tell me?"

He remained silent.

Her hand rose toward his face, hovering, but she didn't touch him. "You are unscarred."

"Yes. The results of your magic."

A long moment passed. Nate's chest burned. Realizing he'd been holding his breath, he released it with a huff.

"I've missed those conversations." Her smile, her expression, was fragile as she stared at him in wonder. "How serendipitous that we should meet again, and I finally learn your fate. Once they transferred you out of my ward, I had no word where you went or how you fared. We rarely do unless the patient writes to us afterward."

"It wasn't chance, Mistress. I was looking for you."

NINE

D arya's pulse roared in her ears.

Her belly flipped one way and flopped another. She thought she recognized his voice but brushed it from her thoughts. Of course, she knew the voice of General Kirin. Anyone who met him wouldn't forget those rich tones.

But he'd reminded her of someone else.

Someone vulnerable and on the fringes of life. An image that a general would never allow.

The one soldier that she let get a hook in her heart. After his transfer, her work, her world became a little grayer. Her ability to fulfil her duty became more challenging.

Her magic began to fail, and she didn't know why.

That kind-hearted soldier. So full of pain and thought. A man with the heart of a bard and a sense of knowing that curled around her soul and knotted.

She hoped he recovered and went onto live his life.

She hoped that for all of her patients.

She hoped *he'd* write to her.

The letters she received from other patients brought her joy.

She hoped to see *him* again.

Sometimes she saw former patients and indulged in a sense of quiet relief that her efforts helped someone.

Deep down, buried further down than any other hope. She hoped for *him*.

As she nursed him back to health, she was sure there had been some magical connection between them that had nothing to do with her ability to heal the body. That secret part of her hoped that maybe this one—this *one* special soldier would be hers.

The one I could give 'forever' to.

Then one day he was gone. No word or letter came. She closed the door and let the earth fall in on that buried hope and got on with life.

As she always had.

Now she searched Nate's face—General Kirin's face. A face she'd seen countless times, but never associated it with her special soldier, bandaged and unknown. The voice of the man she'd fallen in love with belonged to the face of a General that belonged to the empire.

Not to her.

"I'm glad my service was successful." She said, falling into medical protocol while she wrangled her heart into place.

"This is why I didn't tell you who I was. This barrier of duty and rank and protocols. Did you not hear me? It wasn't chance that I was at your path. I was looking for *you*." He sounded exasperated.

She was so busy trying to control her emotions, the meaning of his words floated around her consciousness. "I don't understand."

He stepped closer, fingers extending toward her, but curled back on themselves as he lowered his hands to his sides. His voice was so soft. As soft as it had been when prone on the clearing station cot. "I thought we might revive some of those conversations. They were... special." His eyes searched her face. "At least, they were to me."

She stared at him. The words finally finding their way into her tired brain.

"I understand you may feel differently, after all, there were many soldiers brought through your ward and-"

Thought ceased, and impulse took over, launching herself forward. Her lips on his stopped his words. Too many words. All they had in the past were words.

Pain flared through her chest. Anguish. Joy. Hope. All flared to life at once, threatening to overwhelm her.

His arms encircled her, and tears threatened to spill from eyes that determinedly remained dry for years. Since her youth. Since war had stolen most of her family.

The sensation of his warm lips against hers, his arms around her, was a different sort of magic. A place she wanted to revel in the rest of her days. He held her close, taking over, deepening the kiss. Telling her things that words were too pale to say.

"Darya?" Jeni's weak voice broke the stillness of the night.

Nate's arms released her, lingering, hands caressing her waist as he stepped back. They stared into each other's eyes just a few seconds longer.

He reached for the water bucket and followed her back inside.

The babe slept on Jeni's chest, fists curled up at his chin within the swaddling.

Jeni's skin sheened in the low light of the hearth fire.

Darya's hands were instantly on her, gentle, assessing.

Fever.

Darya's heart rate slowed as she forced herself to think out the next steps.

Nate bathed Jeni's face and neck with a linen and clean water from a wooden bowl while Darya checked the blood-flow. It hadn't eased.

She searched for the *slànachadh bodhaig* flower from her satchel.

Trimming off the proper portions of what she would need from the plant, she dropped it into the small portable mortar and pestle she kept in the satchel when she made visits. As she ground it, she thought of what else she might do, trying not to place too much hope on Tommy's arrival with more medicines. Or, Goddess' luck, a new crystal spoon to amplify what little magic she had left.

Her hands worked while her mind wondered if the broken shards would still work? Would it be enough? She doubted it, but she could try, once she scrubbed the raider's blood from the piece she used to defend herself.

Extracting the shards from the bag, she took the soiled one and set to scrub it, but it wouldn't come clean. Blood remained in the rough crevices of the unpolished stone.

Without knowing what would happen, she couldn't risk using it.

Picking up the other piece of the broken crystal spoon, she rinsed it free of any dust or other potential contaminates until it appeared clean.

Glancing toward her patient, she studied the change in her appearance. Nate held the child, tiny within his hands, peering with wonder into his little face before placing him in the safety of the nearby bassinet.

Darya tipped the ground *slànachadh bodhaig* into one of Jeni's small clay cups and set it aside, then rifled through her bag for other medicines to ease the fever first. But there just wasn't enough of anything useful. A wave of exhaustion and frustration overwhelmed her. She slammed her palms down on the wooden table.

The remaining shard of spoon toppled from the table, shattering further on the hearthstone.

Darya stared in horror.

This damned, endless war was killing everyone with its bony, tendril-curling fingers.

She looked up into Nate's face as his warm hand slid over her shoulder. "Will the flower you found work?"

"I'm not sure. It wasn't mature enough. I can't be sure it has the right qualities needed, or that it would be enough." She stared at her hands. "I don't know if I can do this anymore."

His large hands enveloped hers, thumbs rubbing over the backs of her knuckles.

"What can I do to help?" His voice was soft, drawing her attention to his face. The concern and desire to help etched so deeply into the tired lines of his face touched her.

She worked alone, shouldering the burden of so many lives for so long. That simple question was like a gentle poke to the heart. For the third time this day, she quickly blinked away tears and drew a deep breath.

"Just keep her as comfortable as you can."

He nodded, then drew her into his arms without another word.

The urge to melt into him overwhelmed her. The desire to allow the fear and urgency to flow from her muscles and bones and absorb only the sensation of being supported, just for a few moments, dragged at her.

His soft lips brushed her brow as he released her and returned to Jeni's side.

Darya listened for a moment.

Nate spoke to Jeni, much the same way the ward clerics spoke to their patients. Goddess knew Nate spent enough time in the clearing station to pick up a thing or two.

He drifted back from near death.

Jeni's tired voice murmured the names of her husband and children.

Darya poured hot water from the hearth cauldron into the small cup, positioning herself so that her back was to Jeni's cot.

She spared the broken spoon shard an angry glance, then began the spell.

The magic sparked, weak but coming to life, and began to flow through her fingers.

Nate, keeping Jeni's attention focused, told her of his time in the ward.

"I was a soldier once. Wounded beyond recognition on the field of battle. My face lacerated and burned by an incendiary, I spent an immeasurable amount of time in the field hospitals. We call them clearing stations. And under the care of the most talented ward cleric, I was healed."

Darya listened to his story as she struggled to gather the magic to infuse the *slànachadh bodhaig* tea, bolstering its properties to help save Jeni's life, so that the infant and her other children wouldn't be motherless.

"But it wasn't just this cleric's skill that kept me alive. I was wont to give up many a time. The pain and despair were great. I had nothing to go home to. Nothing to keep me to this world," he said.

Darya's heart hitched at the underlying loneliness in his words.

"It was the gentleness of her touch. More than that, the heart in her voice. She often said she was just doing her duty. But a patient *feels*—or doesn't feel, sincerity, no matter the words. That's when I slid into love with my healer."

"What happened to her after you were mended?" Jeni's weak voice floated to Darya.

"They transferred me to a convalescent ward once they deemed I wouldn't die. And then I lost her."

"Oh, that's so sad."

"Until this very day."

Jeni gasped. "How lovely."

Darya smiled.

That's when I slid into love with my healer.

An influx of battle patients rendered her far too busy and exhausted to think beyond the next life presented to her. She lost many. Too many beyond her ability. And the military, seeing she was no longer healing more than she lost, allowed her discharge from duty. She, too, like many others, was handed a service medal and a pat on the head. That medal bought her tiny cottage.

"In that recovery ward, I heard many, many soldiers talking about their saviours in the clearing stations. How those talented healers saved their lives and how grateful they were for it. Many of them had families to return to. I suspect, were it not for the exhausting efforts of those ward clerics, the lands would be far worse off than they are now. They made all the difference."

"My husband is on the front lines now." Jeni said.

"He will need you on his return."

Jeni murmured something else, but it was too low for Darya to hear.

She closed her eyes, straightened her spine and focused, seeking the root of her magic. This time, when she found it, she could somehow sense that the root was even deeper than she'd previously known and followed it to its core.

Letting Nate's words whisper through her consciousness, she clung to them, trying to coax and build the magic. Trying to find that flare to grasp and bring to the surface.

She recalled the sound of Jeni's voice reciting the names of her children.

She recalled the sound of Nate's voice during their long conversations in the quiet hours of the ward.

The sight of him standing between herself and three would-be attackers, unarmed.

His determination to help her save this woman's life.

The feel of his lips on hers.

His arms around her.

After all this time, he'd come looking for her.

That's when I slid into love with my healer.

Her breath hitched as her hands flared to life. Clutching the cup between them, she directed the magic to boost the healing properties of the *slànachadh bodhaig*.

When her magic didn't sputter or fade, she brought the cup to Nate to administer to Jeni, while Darya quickly got to work on her belly.

Pushing the coverings aside, she slid her hands under the damp chemise and placed them flat on either side of Jeni's bellybutton and closed her eyes.

"What is she doing?" Jeni asked Nate.

"Healing. Drink so you can help her."

Darya spared Jeni a glance.

Jeni stared at her over the rim of the cup, her eyes full of wonder and fear. But there was hope there, too.

Darya closed her eyes, concentrating on guiding the magic to where it needed to go. She couldn't know for certain what was the exact cause of the hemorrhage and fever, she just had to do her best to entice it to find what needed healing and pray to the Goddess the magic was strong enough.

It ebbed.

Perspiration broke out on her brow as she struggled to keep it flowing.

I promised to visit the Temple as soon as possible if the Goddess will just help me heal Jeni.

Her breath shuddered with the effort of holding the magic.

Nate's hand slid over her shoulder. The contact provided the steadiness she needed.

Under her hands, there was a shift in flow and Jeni's muscles tightened under her palms.

Jeni gasped, drawing a deeper breath.

The medicine was easing the pain and fever, giving the body a reprieve, making it easier for the magic to flow through the blood and tissue.

Now was the time to bear down. Much like the birthing process, there was a time to ease and a time to push. Darya pushed her magic, her life force, through her hands, flooding the concentrated area of Jeni's body to knit the wounds and push the beginnings of infection out of her.

If Jeni was the very last patient she could ever heal using magic, then so be it. Her children needed her.

After what seemed like forever, the magic finally flickered.

Never had she pushed so hard, given so much.

On her knees, next to the cot, she sagged as she finally released it. The expected chill followed, gripping her in a deep shudder.

Nate helped her to her feet, guided her to the bench by the table, then disappeared.

He returned bearing a fresh bucket of water from the well, and the ladle, so that she may drink.

"Thank you." She managed, as weary as she was.

"The sun is nearly up."

She looked to the windows, grayer than black now.

"I hope Tommy makes it back safely."

"Laoch will see that he does."

TEN

Laoch's hooves on the packed earthen and cobbled path outside the cottage signalled Tommy's return. The door bounced off the interior wall, followed by the squall of the startled infant as Tommy stood wide-eyed in his home, surveying the room. A satchel slipped from his shoulder to the floor with a muffled thump.

"Wipe the mud from your feet before coming inside," Jeni ordered.

Tommy blinked, finding her in the gloom of the room. His narrow shoulders sagged, and he smiled. He tossed Darya a grin as he moved toward his mother and new brother.

Nate picked up the bag, setting it on the table beside Darya, who immediately rummaged through its contents, pulling neat-

ly labelled packages and durable stoppered
jars.

Darya's breath whooshed out of her.
"Thank Goddess. There isn't any *sàbhaladh
beatha* here but there is more *slànachadh
bodhaig*, which is nearly as good now that
she is stable."

Nate nodded. "The military has been
commandeering as much as can be collect-
ed and produced."

Darya's voice dropped. "Jeni won't be able
to afford it. I have a few coins at home that
will cover her needs, if you can wait till then
for payment." She was writing on a piece
of linen that she used for bundling her dry
herbs.

Turning his attention back to the cot, he
smiled at Tommy's wonder as the newborn
clutched his forefinger.

"I'll tell my aunt that I'm paying for it this
time."

"Tommy." Darya drew his attention as she
rose to her feet to approach Jeni's cot with
the satchel slung over her shoulder. "Listen
carefully. I've portioned out medicine for

your mother. She'll need your and your siblings' help in the next few weeks. The instructions are on the package. Follow them carefully. And ensure there is always fresh water in the house."

Eyes wide, Tommy nodded.

"We will check in with the militia to find out when it will be safe enough to summon the rest of your children." Nate said to Jeni.

"They've captured the raiders, sir." Tommy said. He turned back to his mother. "Ma, I was all night because Mister Kirin gave me his horse to go to the militia and report on the raiders, then go to his shop where his auntie made me stay all the night until morning."

"That's good Tommy. Very good." Jeni said.

"I will return tomorrow. For now, I have to attend to Mister Kirin's aunt."

"Mind your rest Mistress. Thank you for all you've done. And you as well Mister Kirin."

Nate held the door as Darya passed through into the early morning sunshine.

He was weary, Darya must be bone deep exhausted. Approaching Laoch, he ran a hand along his neck before placing the medicine satchels in the saddlebags, then helped Darya up into the saddle, letting his hands linger on her waist, drift down her hip, along her thigh to rest on her knee.

More hooves clamoured into the small clearing outside the house, drew their attention. A green-coated militiaman riding at the fore.

There was a quick exchange of polite morning greeting when the lead militiaman stated his purpose. "The boy, Tommy, reported raiders in the orchard between here and the village. We captured the party, and while scouting, we found the bodies of several others. Two of the captured raiders reported a witch having killed them. His description matched you, mistress."

"I'm not a witch. I'm a midwife."

The militiaman shrugged. "Witch or not, magic users are expected to be registered and on duty working the front lines. Phillibert, go inside and question the household."

"There was no magic used in that attack," Nate said.

A man extracted himself from the group and strode into Jeni's house.

A moment later Jeni's raised voice chased him back out again, red-faced. "The lady of the house said there are no.. uhm.. witches hereabouts, sir."

The militia leader squinted at Darya. He grunted. "I'll be taking her to the outpost in any case. She can deal with the Administrator directly."

"Mistress McLeighan will be going home to bed to rest," Nate said in a voice that brooked no opposition.

Another of the militiamen moved out of the group, eyes on Nate, and made his way toward the militia leader, whispering to him.

"I'm told you are General Kirin."

Nate nodded.

Several other militiamen peered around their comrades, then moved forward, all staring at Nate.

"We served under the General, sir." One said to the leader. "All honourably discharged after our tours of duty and now serve on the home front."

Many of the men looked from Nate to Darya. A few even had tears in their eyes.

"It was an honour serving with you, sir," the speaker said to Nate as they lined up in front of the militia leader's horse to pay their respects.

When they saluted, their eyes moved from Nate to Darya.

Nate returned the veterans' salute.

"Thank you all for your service." Darya said from her position atop Laoch.

The militia leader tipped his hat to Nate, then to Darya before turning his horse and leading the unit back up the path.

"Thank you." Darya's voice was quiet.

Nate looked up.

She stared after the men, her expression far away.

"Looks to me like they remember you." He said with a grin.

"It would seem so. Shall we go?"

"Aye, you need your rest after a night like that."

"As do you. You were a fine assistant. Will you take your rest at my home? It's a long way yet back to yours."

Nate studied her face.

"I think we have much more to discuss of the past," she said.

"And of the future."

"Aye, the future." She nodded, reaching forward to place a hand on his cheek.

He slid his hand over her knee. "Perhaps we can figure out how to replenish your magic."

"It's always there, it just needs the right spark." She said, lips parted, as her eyes roamed his face.

He mounted Laoch and settled into place behind Darya, her back pressed to his front. His arms encircled her. Her hands slid over his, holding him closer.

He hugged her to him, dipping his head to nuzzle her neck, drawing a deep breath. "I've waited so long for this." He whispered next to her ear.

"As have I." She turned so that she could see his face. "Let's go home."

Their lips ghosted then met. Gentle, tentative at first. Her fingers slid along his jaw and he deepened the kiss. Sure. Committed.

At peace.

NEXT...

The Kindred Chronicles

JodiKendrick.com

A new fantasy romance series that starts with the short and sweet story *'Healer'*, then follows with the much steamier full-length novel *'Mercenary'*.

A Fantasy Romance featuring a human mercenary who struggles with her buried past and an elven prince in search of the source of his power after he is removed from the line of succession. Together they will face beastly enemies to save their loved ones - and each other.

THANK YOU!

Dear Reader,

Thank you so much for taking the time to read *Healer*. If you enjoyed it, please consider leaving a review on your favourite platform.

For free downloads, to join my newsletter and browse my growing library for more books with *Romance, Adventure and Passion*, visit **JodiKendrick.com**

-Jodi

Jodi
Kendrick

Jodi Kendrick lives in Eastern Ontario Canada with her *Favourite Person* and chompy furbaby, while their adult children explore the wider world.

As a romance author, she writes in paranormal, fantasy, steampunk & gaslamp subgenres, and sometimes delves into urban fantasy and paranormal women's fiction. Her characters are often quirky, sometimes cranky, but they all woman-up and get the job done while their partners ensure they survive with all their bits and bobs attached.

A history enthusiast and word dabbler most of her life, she enjoys exploring 'beyond-the-everyday' and the 'time-before-now', discovering relationship threads weaving individuals through time and place. She's rarely seen without flashy note-books and colourful pens.

Follow Jodi on Social Media:

SOARING DRAGON

The Soaring Dragon Chronicles

JodiKendrick.com

Love and Adventure aboard the luxury airship The Soaring Dragon.

GPSA

Carson & Lirikai   Ian & Raya   Magnus & Ana   Renni & Pia

The Global Paranormal Security Agency

The *Global Paranormal Security Agency* is a hidden organization dedicated to bridging the paranormal and human worlds to keep everyone safe.

Protect. Defend. Seek Justice.

STAND ALONES

Dragon Island

Enchanted Ardor

JodiKendrick.com

'Dragon Island' and *'Enchanted Ardor'* are the beginnings of two more new series.
More coming soon!

FUCN'A

FUCN'A Series

JodiKendrick.com

EveL Worlds Furry United Coalition
Academy World

FINELY AGED

'Dragon Steel' is an urban fantasy spinoff
from paranormal romance *'Dragon Heat'.*
More *'Finely Aged'* stories coming soon!

Dragon Island
Dragon Heat

Enchanted Ardor
Wish

EveL Worlds : FUCN'A
Tough Nut
Diamond in the Ruff
Honeyed Nut
Gorilla in the Hiss
FUCN'A Collection One
Pedigree Collection

Finely Aged
Dragon Steel

Global Paranormal Security Agency
Awakened
Surfacing
Polestar
Aquatic Investigations
Prowler

The Kindred Chronicles
Healer
Mercenary

The Soaring Dragon Chronicles
Return Flight
Changeling